"A gripping story of life under the brutal regimes of Batista and Castro's Cuba, told with the authenticity of one with firsthand experience of what it was like. Highly Recommended."

Michael Bright, English Professor/Emeritus Professor at Eastern Kentucky University. Author of *Cities Built to Music*.

"A lively and flowing narrative for the wider public about the final days of Fulgencio Batista's dictatorship in Cuba and the radical change that took place on the island in January 1959. The book describes in a testimonial tone and with abundant fictional notes the tense social situation of that time from the perspective of a family of rural owners, descendants of Spanish immigrants. This fine narrative written by Armando González-Pérez is ideologically in tune with other works about the time in which disenchantment becomes evident with the revolutionary changes whose authoritarianism and excesses triggered a dramatic and endless exodus, especially toward the United States."

Armando Chávez-Rivera, Professor of Spanish American literature and culture, University of Houston-Victoria. Member of the North American Academy of the Spanish Language. Author of *Dictionary of Provincialisms of the Island of Cuba*.

"In *Stolen Dreams*, Armando González-Pérez strives to document pre- and post-revolutionary circumstances that brought forth disenchantment for many, as well as the still ongoing volition to migrate. By making his protagonist a promising baseball player, he introduces in the narrative a religious (tone) of sorts, since for countless islanders the sport supersedes the day-to-day, transporting them into a world of make-believe. Into a quasi-Neverland. Unlike, for instance, poet Luis Lorente, who in his "1968" explains that "his passion, baseball," gave way to urgency at a time when "from one day to the next, the stadium awakened transformed into huge cow pastures: firing ranges and training fields for members of the national militia," González-Pérez´s hero never gives up on his quest. Intent on pursuing it in the United States, he takes to the sea with other dreamers.

Although the majority of Cubans who arrived on American shores in 1960 and '61—which is approximately when the story´s denouement transpires—aboard planes after securing visa waivers, others did so by boat, risking a journey that, paradoxically, most viewed almost insurmountable at the time. Of course, later on, particularly after the so-called 1994 raft exodus, the terror of the ocean crossing had vanished. This notwithstanding, González-Pérez´s narrative portrays emphatically a historical moment defined by anguish, desperation, disillusionment and impotence to encounter societal transformation that propelled thousands of Cubans to pursue freedom in other shores. In this sense, Stolen Dreams is at once a work of fiction and an accurate depiction of a dramatic period. The saga´s tragic outcome, somewhat modulated by the survival of a single individual who lives to tell the tale, underscores appropriately the authorial objective to promote pathos and hence induce empathy for his characters and their ... destiny.

Jorge Febles, Professor of Spanish American literature and culture. Emeritus Professor at Western Michigan University and Northern Florida University. Author of *Revisiones: Lecturas heterogéneas de textos Cubanos.*

Published by Mission Point Press
2554 Chandler Rd.
Traverse City, MI 49696
(231) 421-9513
www.MissionPointPress.com

ISBN: 978-1-958363-51-5
Library of Congress Control Number: 2022922124
Printed in the United States of America

DEDICATION

To the memory of my parents, for their love, sweat, and tears in raising me.

To everyone who loves freedom, for it is as precious as life itself.

To my wife, for her love and encouragement in writing this book.

ACKNOWLEDGEMENTS

My appreciation to the following people for their incredible generosity in reading the manuscript of Stolen Dreams and for their valuable comments and suggestions: Jorge Febles, Armando Chávez-Rivera, Chris. W. Weston, Michael Bright, Jenna Mindel, Teresa Dovalpage, and Diana Álvarez-Amell. A nod of thanks to my granddaughter Isabel for her technical help and to the Mission Point Press staff for their professional assistance. Additional gratitude to Anne Stanton for her valuable guidance, expertise, and insight as the copy editor. And finally, this book wouldn't have been possible without the love and encouragement of my wife, Jill.
Blessings to all of you.

"Life without liberty is like a body without spirit."

—Kahlil Gibran, author of "The Prophet"

"Freedom, Sancho, is one of the most precious gifts that heaven has bestowed upon man; no treasures that earth holds can compare with it; for freedom, as for honor, life may and should be ventured ... captivity is the greatest evil that can fall to the lot of man."

—Miguel de Cervantes Saavedra, author of "Don Quijote of La Mancha." Part II / Chapter 58

"Man is Nature's most wonderful creature. Torturing him, crushing him, murdering him for his beliefs and ideas is more than a violation of his human rights—it is a crime against humanity."

—Armando Valladares, author of "Against All Hope"

AUTHOR'S NOTE

Fidel Castro's guerrilla fighters defeated the ruthless dictator Fulgencio Batista y Zaldívar in 1959. Castro's ensuing vengeance against political enemies and takeover of private assets drove hundreds of thousands of Cubans of all walks of life to flee to everywhere in the world, but especially to the United States. *Stolen Dreams* is a heart-rending account of Pablo's life when he was caught in the vortex of violence by two tyrannical governments. Pablo is torn between his dream of playing baseball abroad and his desire to stand up for freedom and justice for all in his homeland. He, like his friends, risks his life attempting to cross the dangerous Straits of Florida to flee oppression and tyranny. As José Martí wrote, "To change masters is not to be free … Man loves liberty, even if he does not know that he loves it. He is driven by it and flees from where it does not exist." *Stolen Dreams* is a tribute to all who have tried and—after six decades—are still attempting to flee to freedom to anywhere by any means.

BIOGRAPHY

 Armando González-Pérez received his doctorate from Michigan State University. He is an emeritus professor at Marquette University where he taught for many years in the Department of Languages, Literatures and Cultures, Co-editor of *Caribe: revista de cultura y literatura* for fifteen years. He has published a number of essential works in the field of Afro-Hispanic research, including many articles and the following books: *An Essential Anthology of Afro-American Poetry*; *Critical Approaches to Afro-Cuban Literature*; *Afro-Cuban Theater of the Diaspora*; *Feminine Voices in Contemporary Afro-Cuban Poetry*. He recently published a poignant and heartwarming story of a dog in search of love: *Chance: From Turkey with Love*.

BIONOTA

Armando González-Pérez recibió su Doctorado (Ph.D.) de Michigan State University. Profesor Emérito de Marquette University. Enseñó por muchos años en la facultad de Lenguas, Literaturas y Culturas de Marquette University. Co-editor de *Caribe: revista de cultura y literatura* por quince años. Ha publicado también numerosos estudios claves sobre la literatura afro-hispana que incluyen artículos y los libros siguientes: *Antología clave de la poesía afroamericana*; *Acercamientos a la literatura afro-cubana: Ensayos Interpretativos*; *El Teatro Afro-Cubano en el Exilio*; *Voces femeninas en la poesía afrocubana contemporánea*. Su publicación más reciente es *Chance: de Turquía con amor*, la fascinante y conmovedora historia trasatlántica de un perro golden retriever en busca de amor y su hogar permanente.

PROLOGUE

Baseball or *pelota*, as it is called in Cuba, is the nation's pastime.† It became Pablo´s passion when his father gave him a glove and a baseball on the celebration day of Epiphany or *Día de los Reyes Magos*. Like most Cuban boys, he dreamed of being the best baseball player he could be. He practiced diligently and played in *pitenes*, pickup games, with his friend Ariel whenever he could. The neighborhood boys showed up at the same time every day, no matter if the sun had scorched the field to brown or rain had turned it to mud. As he grew into his teens, he played for his home team *Alacranes* and then for the sugar mill team of *Central Perseverancia*. The competition became much stiffer than his boyhood sandlot games, but that did not faze him. In fact, he welcomed the challenge for it sharpened his skills. Soon the town of Aguada de Pasajeros was buzzing about his pitching skills and his passion for the game. Old and young raved about his masterful control of the ball—his mean overhand curve ball and sweeping side-arm pitch that mesmerized the batters.

Pablo hoped that someday an American scout would see him pitching and sign him to a Major League farm team. He was sure he had the talent, yet he worried that his goal of playing professionally abroad was just a pipe dream. With the political upheaval raging in the country against President Batista´s brutal regime, nothing was certain— especially leaving Cuba.

†Roberto González Echevarría's book *The Pride of Havana* is a great book about the history of Cuban baseball.

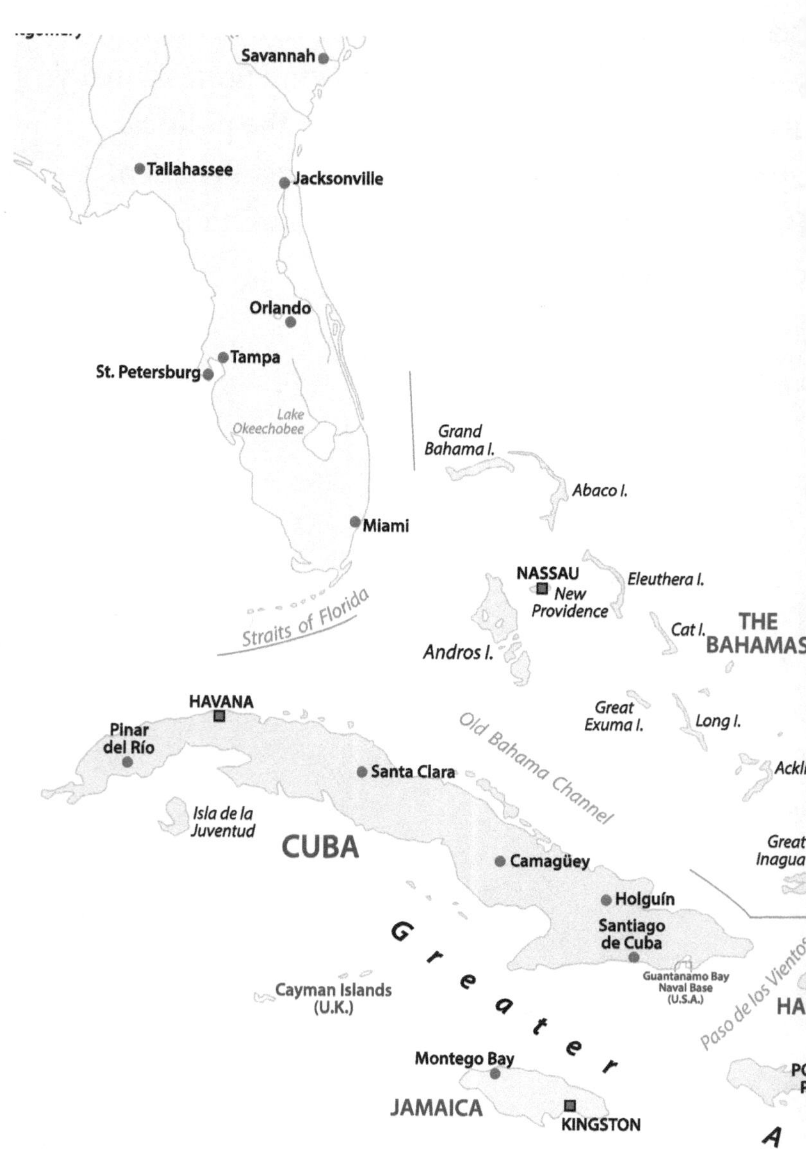

Shutterstock Image

CHAPTER I

Pablo was born in 1941 in *Finca La Aurora*, the farm that belonged to his paternal grandfather, Quintín Ayala Leal. Quintin had left the Galician hills of Spain in the 19th century as an impoverished young man, fleeing famine and political chaos in his homeland. His grandfather, like other immigrants from that part of the world, worked on farms in many parts of the island until he finally settled near the town of Aguada de Pasajeros in the province of Las Villas. There he bought some forsaken land full of *marabú* near a flowing stream in a wooded area. He cleared the weeds and jungle, working from sunrise to sunset. On most nights, he was so exhausted that he went to bed right after dinner. It took him decades to build his home and farm.

Now an old man, he still remembered his harrowing immigration odyssey, and seasons of drought and unending rains. But along with the suffering was Aurora, the love of his life. He loved to reminisce about meeting her in the town's *verbena*.

"Love at first sight," he would say to Pablo, sighing.

But their courtship wasn't all roses. Her mean

father didn't like him and warned her of grave consequences if she continued seeing a poor immigrant unworthy of her family name. But love prevailed and they finally married without her father's blessing. They had three boys. Santiago, the oldest, was Pablo's father.

At age 20, Santiago married Victoria, who had two sons before getting pregnant again with her third, Pablo. Victoria knew the labor pains came too soon—at seven months—and implored Santiago to fetch the old midwife, Julia, who had helped her with the other deliveries.

The birth was difficult. As hours ticked by, Julia encouraged Victoria to relax between contractions, so as not to get exhausted. Finally, after two days, Pablo was born, a puny and silent baby. Most alarmingly, his skin was nearly a bright blue. Julia had to spank him hard several times before they could hear him whimper. Even then, his breathing was labored and he refused to nurse. Julia wrapped him in a soft, colorful blanket and laid him in a crib surrounded with hot stones for warmth. For several days his life hung in the balance until he finally opened his big jet-black eyes, cried mightily, and nursed voraciously. He was so little that they began calling him *Chiquitín*, little one.

CHAPTER II

Pablo's childhood was the opposite of his precarious birth. He was a wiry, healthy, happy, and likable child who grew up to be a fine young man. As the *Benjamín* or youngest son in the family, Pablo was pampered to the envy of his two older brothers. But he was not exempted from his duties on the farm. He was expected to follow in the footsteps of his grandfather and father who viewed farming as a good and healthy way to learn and appreciate what you work for in life. Later, he would remember with nostalgia his pleasant upbringing and his close relationship with his family.

Pablo got along well with his siblings, especially Israel, who was closer in age and his best friend. They were free to roam after a day of hot, hard work. They'd secretly swim in the river or steal a few guavas from a neighbor's tree.

Most importantly, Israel practiced baseball with Pablo whenever he could, patiently teaching his little brother a few tricks about being a pitcher. His sweet mother was the boys' savior, protecting them when they got into mischief. His father was stern and strict but also a kind, fair and a loving man.

Pablo was closest to his father, who watched him with a proud silence at his baseball games. Occasionally, he took him hunting in the Ciénaga de Zapata, a swampy forest teeming with exotic birds and animals. These expeditions were exhilarating but also dangerous because of the muck that could suck you in. And then there were the crocodiles. Once, a big one attacked their loyal dog, Palomo, and then turned and took off after Pablo. Before he could reach him, his father lassoed the croc, turned it over, and killed it with one shot. He then roasted some of the meat. It was tasteless, like the meat of the arboreal jutía, a large rodent that hangs from trees by its tail. Father always kidded Pablo for making faces every time he gave him some to eat by saying *lo que no mata engorda*/What doesn't kill you, makes you stronger. Pablo much preferred the meat of wild quail doves with their sweet berry taste.

CHAPTER III

Neither one of Pablo's parents had much formal education, and they disagreed about his future. His father, with his broad shoulders, piercing blue eyes and leathery skin from working many hours under the tropical sun, wanted Pablo to help his brothers in the field. He felt that Pablo already knew how to read and write, and that was enough. Pablo's father had only known farm life and had a simple and uncomplicated view of life: work hard and respect people and property. His pretty mother, who had curly brown hair and deep black eyes like him, thought otherwise. She wanted him to get the formal education she never received. She insisted that Pablo must continue his schooling whatever else happens. She believed it was the only way to get ahead in life and would talk of nothing else at dinnertime. Finally, his father came around. In fact, he was the one who took him to the *Instituto de Segunda Enseñanza*, a high school in the city of Cienfuegos for a special exam. The written test took hours and the grading even longer. Pablo and his father waited in a hot, high-ceiling gym for the exam results with the other prospective students. Finally, a balding man stood in front of the classroom and called out the names of those who passed. Finally ... "Pablo Ayala Diaz."

Pablo's father was a man of few words and not very demonstrative about his feelings, but that day he beamed with pride and grabbed Pablo in a bear hug.

"Pablo, I am so proud of you. You are the first one in the family to attend high school. You will do well, I know," he said and pulled him close

He took Pablo to eat at the famous Caribe Restaurant, known for its delicious deep-fried red snapper. The next stop was the downtown barbershop, owned by his friend Marcelo Dorta Carvajal.

"Marcelo, this is my youngest son, Pablo. As you can see, a *galleguito* like his grandfather. I am so proud of him. He passed his exam at the Instituto this morning. He will be going to school here. Can you give him a good haircut?"

"Well, of course!" said Marcelo, an outgoing and jovial soul with thinning white hair. "Your son looks to be a fine young man."

Then he turned to Pablo and welcomed him, opening his arms wide in front of the barbershop window.

"Pablo, you are a lucky man to be here! The city

of Cienfuegos is famous for its splendid architecture! Around here, we call it the Pearl of the South."

"My youngest son, Emilio, is also at the Instituto," Marcelo continued. "He will love meeting you. Come on! Let's cut your hair."

Pablo liked Marcelo and listened closely as he talked about Emilio and what was in store for him at the high school. And what a treat to get such a good haircut. Much better than the one his father gave him, although he'd never say that. After leaving Marcelo, he and his father did some window shopping and took the train back home.

The train chugged through the rolling hills of the countryside, dotted with majestic palm trees and large sugar cane fields toward Aguada. Pablo and his father talked about many things, his father always returning to the topic of Pablo's balancing his responsibilities at the farm with playing baseball and going to school so far from home. He would have to take the train or bus home each morning and late afternoon, a ride of at least forty minutes. Pablo understood that from now on he would have to manage his time better. His only free time to play baseball would be after farm chores on weekdays and on weekends.

CHAPTER IV

One Sunday, after pitching a winning two-hit game against a good Calimete team, he met Manuel Rojas, who also went by the name of Manny. He had once been an umpire for a Triple-A League in the States!

When he retired, Manuel returned to Cuba and settled in Aguada to work part-time for the Washington Senators. His job was to identify the top players in Las Villas Province.

Manuel watched Pablo pitch one afternoon and was dazzled by the speed of his pitches. He was young, he thought, but brimming with potential. But it was clear that he needed to learn how to read the batter. Pablo approached every batter with the same few pitches. After he introduced himself after the game, he told him about Mr. Cambria, a scout for the Washington Senators.

"He is looking to recruit our top players. I'm going to ask him to come see you pitch before he returns to the United States. He's scouting Zoilo Versalles in Havana." Pablo was elated to be considered alongside Versalles, one of Cuba's greatest players who became a top shortstop for the Minnesota Twins.

Lo and behold, Cambria came two weeks later to watch Pablo pitch a brilliant four-hit game, defeating a star-studded team from Cienfuegos. He was impressed by Pablo's demeanor, composure and, of course, his pitching skills. But he still felt that Pablo would be more dominant by adding another pitch to his repertoire like a mean slider. He also needed to get stronger. Pablo was just a sixteen-year-old teenager whose uniform hung on his skinny body. Manuel promised Cambria he'd keep him informed of his progress.

Pablo was elated about his evaluation, but disappointed about having to wait another year. Deep in his heart, he felt he was already pitching at a higher level. But he managed his emotions, telling himself he wouldn't let this temporary setback get him down. He had to rise above the occasion. As the year progressed, Manuel, a man of humble origin like him, became a friend and a mentor. As a former umpire, he knew exactly what to say to help Pablo refine his skills as a pitcher. He focused especially on what to look for when facing a batter. How close or far he is to the plate and if he crouches or stands straight. But above all, he advised him to study the batter's strengths and weaknesses.

"Pablo, be sure to pay attention to whether he is a power hitter or a speedster who slaps the ball. Don't forget that the most important thing is to disrupt his timing, to keep him guessing."

As Pablo became stronger, his pitches became even faster and more controlled. Somehow, it translated to his schoolwork, especially math. Instead of giving up in frustration, he would give himself more time to study, to understand a problem instead of going through the steps. His grades soared.

CHAPTER V

But around him, the political situation was affecting his friend Ariel and his family. Ariel's father, like many seasonal workers, could not find a job during the *tiempo muerto* or dead season when the sugar mills shut down. In order to survive, the workers frequently mortgaged their next year's wages, buying their food on credit at a landowner's *bodega* where they were often cheated. The corrupt politicians did nothing to help; the wealthy didn't care for them either.

Ariel's family was barely making it. After Pablo told his father of their hunger and desperation, Santiago hired them to do some work around the farm in exchange for vegetables and rice.

One night after working all day under a blistering sun, Ariel told Pablo that *guajiros* across the country were being exploited. They could barely survive when the *zafra*, the sugar cane harvest, stopped. They were exploited, he said, and nothing would change until Batista and his corrupt cronies were gone.

Pablo knew that plans for a revolution were afoot, but his father repeatedly told him to never get involved in politics. It could only lead to trouble. Yet his father had also told him to care about others, and he frequently heard his mother repeat the proverb *Haz el bien, y no mires a quién* / Do what is right, come what it may.

Pablo felt torn. He saw for himself the mansions and cars of the wealthy and the suffering of the very poor. He wanted to work for justice and freedom, but what if it jeopardized his baseball career? More importantly, he didn't want to upset his father. After some soul searching, he decided to talk to his friend Emilio, whom he suspected was already conspiring against the government. He approached him in the hallway before going into his world history class.

"Emilio, wait a minute. I need to talk to you. It is very important."

"What's up, man? Trouble with your girlfriend or with the math teacher?" Emilio asked.

"I don't have a girlfriend and I'm doing pretty well in math," Pablo answered.

"What do you mean you don't have a girlfriend? I'm sure you are very popular back home as a ballplayer. Besides, girls must be flocking around you. I heard that Violeta is crazy about you. Haven't you noticed how she looks at you? She melts around you. Wake up, brother!"

"Look Emilio. I am very busy helping at the farm, playing baseball, and going to school here. I don't have time to mess around with girls. There is a time for everything in life and right now I want to be the best baseball player I can be."

"On the other hand, I'm really upset."

He glanced around to see if anyone was listening. You could never tell who a government tattletale might be.

"Look, my friend's family opened up my eyes about the injustice in Cuba, and I want to help them, help all the working poor. But my dad tells me not to get involved. He is stubborn at times, but he is a good father. Can we go someplace to talk about it?"

Emilio suggested the schoolyard or a restaurant in town.

"Okay. Let's get out of here. We can go to La *Cueva Pizzeria* where we can't be overheard. Do you mind if my girlfriend, Teresita, joins us?"

"Is she reliable?"

"Of course, she is reliable," Emilio said, annoyed with his question. "I trust her completely. She hates the political corruption too. Let's pick her up at her art class on our way to the pizzeria."

Teresita was slim, pretty and tall and carried herself with perfect posture. Pablo was impressed with her charm and intelligence. There were a few customers when they arrived at La *Cueva Pizzeria.* They chose a table at the far end. After joking and talking for a while, their conversation focused on the repressive political situation in the country and what to do about it. They had to change their conversation every time they were interrupted by other students, fearing a *soplón* could be among them.

CHAPTER VI

Pablo confided that he wanted to take action but it might dismantle his baseball career and upset his father.

"My father believes that the politicians are corrupt, but his only answer is to stay as far away from them as possible," Pablo said.

"That's not enough," Emilio raised his voice, his temper heating up. "If you remain silent and do nothing, you become part of the problem. Look Pablo, we cannot stand on the sidelines any longer. I know you love baseball and you don't want to get your father angry at you. But even he realizes the politicians are corrupt and violent. We have to do something to change the whole government. It's not just the guajiros who can barely survive. Freedom doesn't exist anymore. People are afraid. Persecutions and abuses are the order of the day. People are increasingly outraged that while they struggle to buy a loaf of bread, the wealthy and the politicians don't give a damn about their struggles. We are committed to the defeat of this tyrannical government."

"But what can I do?" Pablo asked.

"You could start by distributing propaganda leaflets. And later, you could sell bonds to raise money to help topple this miserable government. You would be a great asset in the rural area, but you must be discreet and extremely careful. There are too many chivatos everywhere. We have quite a few here at school. Watch out for the math teacher! She is one of them and she would turn on you in a blink of an eye."

"Do your parents know you're doing this?" Pablo asked.

"My parents have no idea," Teresita said. "I never whisper a word about my feelings about the government."

"My parents do know," Emilio said. "In fact, my dad supports me. He fought during the Spanish Civil War on the Republican side against Francisco Franco and hates any dictator, no matter what country. He thinks it's time to step up against tyranny again."

Pablo was moved by his friends' honesty, and courage. He agreed to distribute the propaganda leaflets now. If all went well, he'd also raise some money by selling bonds. Pablo was aware he had just made a dangerous decision, but had decided life was more than just his baseball career and his father's disappointment.

After leaving the pizzeria, Emilio and Teresita went back to school. Pablo walked to the José Martí Park to take the next bus to Aguada. He couldn't miss it. His brother Israel would be waiting for him to go back to the farm on horseback.

While waiting for the bus, he met an old lady named Guillermina, a priestess of *santería*, the Afro-Cuban Religion. She was a follower of the goddess Oshún and told him all about her.

When he arrived in Aguada, Israel was waiting for him. On the way home, he told Israel about meeting Guillermina, but Israel said he didn't care to hear another word about her beliefs. As a matter of fact, he told Pablo to be careful when talking to strangers.

CHAPTER VII

After getting the leaflets from Teresita, he began distributing them individually or leaving a bunch of them in places where the wind would blow them around and people would read them. One Sunday after a ball game, while talking to his umpire friend about his pitching performance, he brought up the political situation and wondered whether it would stop Cambria from coming back to see him again. Manuel assured Pablo that he had been in touch with Cambria and had told him about his progress as well as the political turmoil going on in the country. As far as he knew, Cambria was planning to come back the following year. Then Pablo took a chance and gave him a leaflet. Manuel's reaction was one of surprise and bewilderment. He took Pablo aside and lectured him.

"What in hell are you doing man? Why are you taking such a fucking risk? If I were an informer, you would be taken to jail and beaten. I admire your conviction and courage, but stop this idiocy. Don't try to give one to your manager. He is suspected to be an informer. Don't ruin your future. You have the talent to be somebody special in baseball. Okay?"

They walked toward Pablo's father, who was chatting and drinking a beer with other fans.

"Does your father know what you're doing," Manuel whispered.

"Of course not. I haven't told him anything. Even though we are close, I fear he'd condemn me."

"If you're not open and honest with him, you might lose him," Manuel said. "It would be far worse if he finds out from somebody else. Then he would feel that you betrayed him and don't trust him at all."

CHAPTER VIII

It wasn't long before the dreaded confrontation took place. Pablo had gone into the kitchen to grab a bite before taking the bus to school. His mother handed him a cup of hot coffee and looked at him grimly.

"Pablo, you are not going to school today," she said. "Your father wants to talk to you after you finish feeding the animals. We will be waiting for you in the dining room,"

After finishing up his chores—cleaning the barn and feeding the pigs—Pablo walked into the dining room where his father and mother were waiting for him. He knew from their faces that something was wrong. His loving mother looked disappointed, and his father was drumming his fingers heavily on the table. His father ordered him to sit near him. As he pulled the leaflet from his shirt pocket, he told Pablo to listen carefully to what he was about to say. How could he not, Pablo thought. His father was nearly shouting.

"Pablo, where in the hell did you get this propaganda leaflet? Who gave it to you? I need a good explanation right now."

Pablo was annoyed and decided it was time to be

honest about his contempt for the government.

"The government is repressive, corrupt and greedy, and it's time we get rid of it. I got the leaflet from Emilio's girlfriend, Teresita. They're both committed to the anti-government movement at school and so am I. But I only help a little by distributing a few leaflets to people I can trust, or I leave them in places for people to read. More and more people are supporting the underground movement. They love freedom, the freedom we don't have right now."

"Look Pablito," said his mother, soothingly and touching his arm, "the Lord sometimes acts in mysterious ways. Sometimes he even uses Satan to further his providential promises."

But Pablo's father could not believe what he was hearing. His son Pablo was involved with an underground movement despite his advice?

"My dear son, have you lost your mind? Think carefully about what you have just said. You are putting yourself and everyone in this household in danger. You know what will happen to you if you ever get caught? To begin with, you will be put in jail. God knows what can happen to you there. Then, they will come for us. By the way, have you heard what happened to your friend Ariel? He is in jail! He has been accused with other boys of writing anti-government graffiti at the Aguada train station. We all know that he doesn't have the education to have done it, but they put him in jail anyway. Someone else wrote the graffiti and ran away. His father Hilario is so upset. He came by yesterday to see if I could help him. Now you are telling us that you are distributing anti-government leaflets? Do you want to be in Ariel's situation? It could happen to you too. Think about it."

His father raised his voice even more, if that was even possible, and demanded that Pablo stop cooperating at once with Emilio and his girlfriend. But Pablo continued pleading his case.

"Father, this is an evil government. We need a new one." Seeing his father's impassive face, Pablo tried a different tactic.

"Well, you know your good friend Marcelo? He agrees with us!"

Instead of persuading his father, it made him even angrier, if that was even possible. Santiago's face turned beet red, and he pounded the table, bang!, with his fist. Pablo flinched.

"Marcelo's support of his son is not my concern! I don't care what he thinks. Emilio is Marcelo's problem. It is not the first time he has faced this situation. It runs in the family. But you are my son. I am telling you now to quit or else there will be dire consequences. Pablo, look at your mother. She is in tears. You tell me you love baseball. Well, are you willing to throw away your future and ruin us too? Ponder it."

Pablo was devastated by his father's reaction. He felt he was too old for that kind of scolding but out of respect for his father he remained quiet. He knew he was partially right, but he stopped arguing for the sake of peace in the family. Furthermore, he wouldn't put his family in danger. It also upset him to hear that his baseball buddy Ariel was in jail. He agreed with his father that Ariel couldn't have written the graffiti. What they had done to him was a clear injustice. What would happen to him now? To his family? Wasn't this proof that it was time to finally get into the fight? Pablo was in turmoil. He took a deep breath.

"Okay father. We agree, at least, that we have an oppressive and an evil government that works for the rich to make them even richer, and that we need to have peace and justice for everyone. Let's see how things shape up. I will stop distributing leaflets. As you say, family comes first and love is above politics. I love you all very much. Okay?"

His parents were relieved by his decision. They stood and embraced him tenderly in a family hug.

CHAPTER IX

Back in school, Pablo told Emilio and Teresita about his tense conversation with his parents. They felt bad for him, and Emilio advised him to quit and lay low for now.

Several weeks later tragedy struck. As he always did, Pablo boarded the bus to go to school on the morning of Thursday 5, 1957, not knowing there was an uprising in the city of Cienfuegos. At dawn, Lt. Dionisio San Roman Toledo led his fellow navy officers in an attack of the southern Naval District. They were joined by the July 26 Movement revolutionaries. The revolt spilled into the city where the rebels, helped by the people, captured important military installations.

Unaware of what was happening, Pablo did his homework during the trip and read an interesting article about the great Martín Dihigo, his favorite baseball player. As the bus approached the José Martí Park at about 9:30 on this tragic day, the bus driver suddenly became agitated, stopped the bus, and screamed at the riders to get out. There was a lot of commotion in the streets. People were milling around shouting *libertad* while gun shots were heard.

The passengers ran in different directions looking for cover. Pablo had planned to go to the Instituto, but on second thought, it could be a dangerous place now. Besides, it would be closed anyhow. He was shocked and scared. He finally decided to look for the barbershop of his father's friend Marcelo. He was not sure of its location but remembered it was close to downtown. It had been a long time since he was there, but he would try to find it.

After looking around and hiding when gunshots rang out, he finally found it on Prado Avenue not far from City Hall. He hoped that Marcelo would be there. The lights were turned off, but he still rapped at the door frantically and called Marcelo's name several times. He was about to leave, when to his surprise the door opened slowly and Marcelo appeared.

"Pablo, my son, what are you doing here? It is providence that you found me. ¡*Entra*! It is dangerous out there. I was about to open the place when all hell broke loose. I heard on the radio about an uprising. Skirmishes have broken out all over the city. The government troops are shooting at people at random with real bullets. They are killing many people and injuring others. Let's get out of here before it gets worse. Come on! I have my old Chevrolet Bel Air parked behind the barbershop. Luckily, Emilio is at home today. He didn't feel well and decided to miss school."

Pablo was so thankful to have found Marcelo, but he worried about his family. He asked Marcelo if he could contact his parents.

"Is there any way you could help me reach my parents? They must be sick worrying about me. My dear mother is surely a wreck."

"Pablo it will be tough, but I will try," Marcelo said without mincing words. "Communication is very sporadic. All the traffic coming into and leaving the city has been stopped but I think the trains are still going. My friend Rigoberto works as a porter. Maybe he could help us. We will stop at the train station on the way home."

At the train station, Pablo stayed in the car while Marcelo talked to his friend Rigoberto to see if he could deliver a message to his friend Santiago.

"It will be difficult, but I'll try," he promised.

Marcelo slipped him a piece of paper that said Pablo was safe and staying with him.

From there, Marcelo drove to his house in the nearby neighborhood of Buena Vista. He pulled into a paved driveway protected by a high iron gate. He got out and unlocked it and drove up to a nice two-story, white house made of cement with beautiful blue Spanish tiles. The house had a small front patio and a spacious garage. As soon as they arrived, Marcelo parked the car, locked the gate, and rushed toward the house followed by Pablo. As he turned the key and opened the front door, he yelled: "*Mi amor*, I am back." His wife, Carmen, heard him and hung up the phone. She raced out the door so fast she nearly collided with him. They hugged and kissed. She asked why it took him so long to get back home after she called.

"Marcelo, my dear, I've been worried about you and Julio and Gustavo! I was just talking with them when you came in. They decided to stay with their uncle Vicente. There hasn't been any disturbance in Rodas. They are safe there with my brother. Thank God! Guess what? I was called from the Sugar Refinery Office that I don't have to go back to work due to the disturbance. Isn't that great! Now I can stay with you all."

"Sorry honey," Marcelo said. "I stopped at the train station to send a message to the parents of Pablo, this fine young man. Do you remember his father,

Santiago? You met him and his wife, Victoria, a while ago."

"Yes, but what's going on?"

"Well, Pablo comes to school every day by bus all the way from Aguada. He said that as the bus approached the José Martí Park this morning, the driver kicked the riders out and sped away. What an irresponsible thing to do, but he was fortunate to find me. I was about to leave the barbershop after hearing on the radio about the disturbance. Pablo is a friend of Emilio. Speaking of Emilio, we should let him know his friend is here."

"How nice you are with us Pablo," said Carmen, wanting first to put Pablo at ease. She was a slender woman with long brown hair and expressive, amber-colored eyes who looked younger than she was.

"I remember your father. Your parents were so kind. They invited us to visit the farm any time to experience real life in the countryside. You can stay with us as long as you want. Marcelo will keep trying to reach your parents. I know that I would be a basket case in their situation. Emilio will be happy to see you. Let me call him. Emiliooo! Emiliooo! Come down. Your friend Pablo is here. Come down!"

CHAPTER X

Pablo met Emilio at the bottom of the stairs, noticing that his friend didn't look all that sick. He told him what happened when he was dropped at the Martí Park and how his father had saved him. Emilio was furious for skipping school due to a migraine. He wished he had been downtown or at school.

"I was just trying to reach Teresita but she's not answering the phone. I'm worried, to tell you the truth."

As they were about to sit down for a hearty and savory Cuban meal, they heard people calling Emilio's name and banging furiously at the gate. Marcelo and Emilio went out to see who was creating such a commotion. It was Teresita and she looked awful, her face streaked with a film of dust and tears. She was accompanied by Rafa, another of their friends. As soon as Marcelo opened the gate, Teresita and Emilio ran toward each other and embraced. Then they all went inside into the living room, where she told them between sobs about her ordeal at school that morning.

"Emilio, I looked all over for you. I was so upset when I couldn't find you. I called you from the school phone several times, but it rang busy or I was disconnected. Then Rafa, Antonio, and I joined a crowd shouting *libertad, libertad*.

"The situation got out of hand. The police arrived, shouting at us to go home. They tried to break up the demonstration with tear gas, but it didn't work. When we kept screaming at them, bullets began flying even though we didn't have any weapons. They shot at us, they were trying to kill us! We ran for cover, but a bullet hit Antonio. He was like a brother to me, Emilio! He fell down and his head was bleeding like crazy. Bastards! They killed him. They killed him! I feared for my life and hid for about an hour at Violeta' house until I was sure it was safe to come out. I wondered whether you could have been arrested or hurt too. I was scared. I had to find you. I thought your parents might know where you were. This is why I came looking for you here. I haven't called my parents or been home either. I don't want to compromise them. They don't know I'm involved with the underground movement."

Carmen sat down next to Teresita and embraced her tenderly.

"Teresita, sweetheart, you are family. We support you. You can stay with us as long as you want, but you have to call your parents now. They need to know your whereabouts. What is their phone number? I will call them right away. If I suspect any problem, I will hang up right away. Is that okay with you?" Carmen asked.

Teresita shook her head yes, and Carmen got up to dial the phone. After a couple of rings, she heard a woman answer.

"*Dígame*, hello. Who is calling please?"

"Mrs. Robles, my name is Carmen Dorta. I am calling because your daughter, Teresita, is a friend of our son Emilio. She is with us now. Do you want to talk to her?"

"Yes. Please put her on," she answered.

"Teresita, my baby, where have you been? We have been looking for you everywhere! Your father even drove to school looking for you. It was closed, but there were still several soldiers stationed there. We miss you. Please come home soon."

"*Mima*, don't worry," Teresita said. "I am with good friends here. Tell Papa I am fine. I will be home later this afternoon. Much love and kisses. Bye mom."

Then she handed the phone back to Carmen.

"Mrs. Robles, please don't worry," Carmen said. "Teresita really is fine. You have an adorable daughter.

We will take good care of her. We will bring her home after lunch."

Everyone was tense. All anyone could talk about at lunch was the uprising. Before taking Teresita back home, they gathered around the television and listened to the official news reports, knowing they were biased. But it was true that the early success of the uprising had crumbled. The government forces had captured the revolutionary officers and then strafed and bombed various neighborhoods killing and maiming civilians. Everyone was afraid. They could hear low-flying planes all afternoon. When Emilio asked if he could go downtown with Rafa, Marcelo objected. It was still too dangerous despite what they heard.

"Tell you what. You can ride with me when I take Teresita home," he said.

Emilio and Pablo took him up on his offer, but Rafa walked home alone. The following morning, Marcelo took Pablo to the train station to catch the next train to Aguada. He talked with Rigoberto who told him that the message had been delivered and answered. Pablo's parents would be waiting for him at the station.

CHAPTER XI

As the train pulled slowly into the train station in Aguada, Pablo could see his parents waving at him. As he stepped out, they came running to meet him. They hugged and his mother, tears streaming down her face, thanked *La Virgen de la Caridad del Cobre*, Cuba's patron saint, for protecting her son.

"Pablito, my Chiquitín, let me hold you tight. I am so happy you are back home and nothing has happened to you. Thanks to Cachita. I kept praying to her to protect you. I have to light more candles to her."

His father, less expressive, patted him on his shoulder.

"Pablo, I am happy you came back unhurt. You were fortunate, you know, and so lucky to find Marcelo. I got his message. What a relief! Let's go and get the horses. I left them tied under a mango tree not too far from here."

On their ride home, Pablo spoke about what happened. He told them about the mayhem in downtown Cienfuegos and Teresita's horrifying experience at school where she saw one of her best friends killed. When they arrived at the farm, it was like the return of the prodigal son. As they dismounted, his siblings ran toward Pablo screaming jubilantly. His dog, Palomo, barked happily and ran to him as he always did when Pablo got home from school. Then they went into the house where his mother had prepared a delicious meal to celebrate the occasion. It was an exhilarating and joyful time of thanksgiving for his return home unharmed.

During the meal, his siblings peppered him with questions.

"Pablo, were you scared shitless when you were dropped at the park with all the shooting going on?" his older brother Alberto asked.

"Of course, I was afraid. I almost peed my pants," he answered. Everyone roared with laughter.

"What do you expect? I was scared and needed to find a place to hide. I remembered that father had taken me to his friend Marcelo's barbershop once. I looked for it until I found it."

As Pablo continued recounting his ordeal, his father remarked that politics was the art of deception and to beware of rotten politicians. Pablo, who was emotionally drained, stared at his father. He would have liked to say something about this comment, but he decided to remain silent out of respect.

CHAPTER XII

The government crackdowns increased after the uprising. Pablo's return to school was doubtful. People were scared to death. They feared that they might be the next target. Pablo's father told him he was able to get his friend Ariel out of jail, but he wouldn't be playing baseball for a while.

"Why?" Pablo asked.

"Ariel is hurt," his father said, not meeting his eyes.

"Father, what do you mean he is hurt? What did they do to him? Pablo asked.

"They beat him up. They broke his fingers so he wouldn't write any more anti-government graffiti. It is cruel what they did to him, but at least he is out of jail and alive," his father answered.

Pablo was livid and shook his fists in anger.

"Damn them! ¡*Cabrones*! When are they going to stop their abuses? It has got to end."

His father understood his rage and tried to hug him. Pablo pulled away.

"Father, is it possible for me to visit Ariel?"

"Why don't you wait for a few days? Ariel probably wants to be with his family now. Give him some time."

After several weeks, Ariel showed up at one of Pablo's home team practices, but, of course, he couldn't participate. He was too injured. The moment Pablo saw Ariel, he stopped pitching and ran to meet him.

"Keep going," he shouted to his teammates. "I need to talk to Ariel."

He walked toward Ariel, his arms open for a hug, but gasped when Ariel smiled at him. Three of his front teeth were missing and his hands were wrapped in heavy gauze.

"Ariel, my buddy, I am so happy to see you again, but wow man! You are so beat up. You can trust me brother. What happened?" Pablo asked.

The two friends walked toward a bench, Ariel limping, to talk out of earshot of the rest of the players.

Ariel's voice choked as he began talking about his nightmare.

"They accused me of writing anti-government graffiti. You know that it's a damn lie. I can't even write most of those words. How could I have done it? I was there out of curiosity. You know, messing around with the guys. I never thought they were doing anything bad. Then, out of nowhere three soldiers appeared shouting at us to stop. The other guys ran away in all directions. I didn't because I hadn't done anything wrong. But that didn't matter. They grabbed me and accused me of being the ringleader. Then one of them squeezed the back of my neck and spat on my face and screamed, 'You so-of- a-bitch. You are their ringleader. You have been writing this damn graffiti all over town!'

"I kept telling them I couldn't write those words if I wanted to. That I flunked most of my classes. But they didn't care. They said, 'Shut up! ¡*Vamos*!' and handcuffed me and took me to their military barracks. Then they took me to the jail and beat me. They broke my fingers with their billy clubs when I tried to protect my face. They kept punching me and laughing until I passed out. When I woke up, I could hardly stand up. I lost three teeth from fist blows. Look at my swollen left knee. It hurts like hell. I don't think I will be able to play with you anymore. I am so lucky that your father got me out of that hellhole. Otherwise, I would be dead by now."

Then, Ariel lowered his voice.

"Pablo, I have to get away. I am a marked man. I will join the rebels in the mountains before the soldiers come back again for me."

Pablo's stomach churned with rage.

"Ariel, I totally understand. It is despicable beyond comprehension what those *canallas* did to you. They will pay for their brutality. My friend be extra careful who you talk to. Here comes Efraim. Be quiet."

"Hey, Ariel, I heard you had some trouble with the law. You look bad, dude. What happened to your fingers? Did you fall or have an accident?" his teammate asked.

"I didn't fall. I had a scuffle with a soldier. I hurt my fingers, but I am okay," Ariel said to deflate the situation.

"Ariel, you better watch out who you go around with. We have too many nutcases lately creating problems. Look what happened in Cienfuegos recently. Pablo was there. I am sure he must have told you about it," he said looking at Pablo suspiciously.

Efraim left and Pablo waited until he was out of earshot.

"Watch out for guys like him, Ariel. He is the proof. Look over your shoulder, man. Be alert and lay low. Feel free to stop by any time. I will be working at the farm or practicing with the team."

CHAPTER XIII

There was tension everywhere. At bus stops, in stores, people said little to each other, not knowing who to trust. Clandestine anti-government groups carried out bold attacks all over the country, especially in Santiago de Cuba, Santa Clara and Havana. Pablo felt tense, even among his teammates. He wondered why his friend and mentor, Manuel, had not come to see him pitch lately and Ariel hadn't called on him.

Then, one night after supper, he learned what happened to them. His father told him that he heard from a friend that Ariel had left for the mountains to fight and Manuel was in jail.

Pablo groaned in anger.

"I wish I had the courage of Ariel! How long are we going to let this go on!"

"Pablo, I understand how angry you are," his father said gently, "but don't do anything foolish. We have to have hope. Fear not. This difficult situation will pass and everything will be okay."

"Father, how are things going to get better? Batista's henchmen are on the warpath. Manuel is in jail! Who is next? Have you heard anything from

Marcelo? I fear for Emilio and Teresita. I am so pissed off. I don't know what to think anymore. It shows in how I am playing lately. I lost the last two games because I was thinking too much. I couldn't concentrate. It has to stop."

Pablo left his father and went for a walk with Palomo as he thought what to do next. The following months were torture, as he debated constantly in his head whether to join Ariel in the mountains or play baseball and continue his education. It was a tough decision to make. His mother pleaded with him to go back to school and finally he relented, but his return was bittersweet. He was happy that nothing had happened to Emilio and Teresita, but the atmosphere on campus was even worse than before the uprising. Soldiers were posted at school and informers were planted in some of the classrooms. When he told Emilio about Ariel's nightmare, he wasn't shocked about the beating he suffered at the hands of Batista's goons.

"Pablo the same thing happened to Rafa, whom you met during the uprising. He survived too. He was lucky. His parents got him out of the country. He is now living with some relatives in Veracruz. Are we next in line? I have thought about joining the rebels in the mountains, but I am more an urban guerrilla man. Pablo, what about you?"

"I have thought seriously about fighting with Ariel in the mountains, but I promised my mother to finish school first. I guess I will have to be an urban guerrilla like you," he said laughing and poking Emilio on the chest.

CHAPTER XIV

The persecution by the government continued unabated as the protests, demonstrations, and attacks by the underground became more frequent. Likewise, the government forces were beginning to suffer losses in the mountains at the hands of the rebels. Life was chaotic, but people were not afraid anymore. The end was in sight. Revolución meant freedom.

On the morning of January 1, 1959, Pablo rushed screaming into the kitchen, where his mother was preparing breakfast. "He is gone. He ran away." He had just heard on his transistor radio that the much feared and ruthless dictator Batista had fled the country to the Dominican Republic. Pablo hugged his mother and asked where his father was.

"He is working in the field. Go and tell him the good news," she said and kissed him on the forehead. Pablo ran to find his father tilling the field near the brook as he prepared the land for planting rice.

"Father, father, he is gone!" Pablo shouted. Batista left the country with his family. The Revolución had won. No more persecution! No more fear! We are free at last."

He was so happy that he jumped up and down and did a silly dance. His father stopped ploughing, removed his hat, and brushed beads of sweat from his brow as he watched Pablo's excitement.

"Son, what did I tell you?" he said. "Governments come and go. You have to be careful not to be enticed by their short-lived power. Politics can be dangerous with its ups and downs. Hopefully we will have a lasting peace now and learn to live with each other in harmony. There has been much fear and suffering for all of us," he said, again wiping the sweat from his forehead.

"Can we go into town to celebrate with everyone else?" Pablo asked?

His father's mouth tightened.

"Pablo, maybe we could go this afternoon after finishing ploughing. Son, we have to be careful that is not a ruse, a lie, to get people to come out. Then you know what will happen. We all will be in jail or dead."

"But father, please listen to the radio. It is true. It is true!"

Later that afternoon, his father relented and rode into town with his two sons on horseback. A big celebration was going on in the streets when they arrived. It was awesome seeing so many people of all ages and social classes cheering, clapping, hugging, kissing and shouting 'Libertad, down with Batista's *esbirros*!' A few gunshots were also heard, not too far away. Pablo saw his father flinch.

Pablo spotted Manuel in the jubilant crowd and waved at him to join them.

"Manuel, what a relief to see you alive. I knew you had been detained and I was worried about you. As you know, my friend Ariel was really hurt in jail."

"Pablo, I did know. I was lucky that I wasn't beaten as severely as he was. I wouldn't have survived at my age. I still have red welts over my body from their damn billy club. They mostly interrogated me. They kept asking me questions about my relationship with you. They wanted to link you to the underground movement, but they struck out with me—no pun intended," he said, laughing.

"I told them about coaching you, making you a better pitcher, but absolutely nothing else. Luckily, your uncle Rogelio was there. He told the other goons that I was harmless. Not to worry about me. Pablo, can you believe what is happening? What joy! Look how happy everyone is. We don't have to be afraid anymore. You can now concentrate on baseball and fulfilling your dream."

Pablo's father and brothers came over and they chatted for a while. Pablo bragged about his brother Israel's baseball skills.

"Manuel, my brother Israel is the really good baseball player in the family. He taught me a lot before he cut his pitching hand tendons cutting sugar cane. Otherwise, he would be playing at least Triple A baseball by now."

Israel beamed, hearing Pablo's praise. His eyes moistened and he squeezed his younger brother's shoulder. They left Manuel to celebrate and went to get the horses to ride back home.

CHAPTER XV

The euphoria they had witnessed lasted for several days. Cuba was having a big *pachanga*. It reached its crescendo when Castro rode triumphantly into Havana with the *barbudos,*rebel forces, on a tank flanked by two of his most trusted generals, Camilo Cienfuegos and Huber Matos.

Ironically, these two revolutionary leaders, in time, were disposed of and discarded. The charismatic Cienfuegos was on a flight to Havana when his plane mysteriously disappeared into the sea. Matos was accused of treason in a kangaroo court and incarcerated for twenty years for questioning the Communist leanings of the Revolution. His trial and others were televised for months and some people shouted *paredón*, meaning "wall"—to the wall to be shot.

"The *Revolución* has turned out to be not what people fought for and expected," Pablo said to his mother after watching the hearings one afternoon in Aguada.

Pablo's own uncle in-law Rogelio was murdered just a month before—beaten and dragged through the streets by a crazy mob that saw him as a hated Batista goon.

"The Revolution has become like the Roman god Saturn, who devoured his own sons for fear of being dethroned by them," Pablo said with discuss.

"It is true, Pablo," she said. "I am still grieving for your uncle Rogelio. Your aunt Josefa must suffer now with this bloody, horrible memory. She will never understand why. He was a good man. He had helped so many people in trouble like your friends Ariel and Manuel."

His aunt Josefa had been so fearful they might come for her family that she had decided to move to a different city. She had stayed with Pablo's family for a few days after the murder and then left with her teenage son Felipe to live in Cárdenas with her other sister Pascuala.

People began to question the Revolución as more civil rights began to disappear and the kangaroo court trials continued being televised. There was so much hate and vengeance. The reprisals were ferocious. Pablo began to understand his father's advice about the perils of politics, especially when there is no democracy. When Pablo spoke to Emilio at school about his concern, he was surprised to hear what he had to say.

"Pablo, Pablo, you are not the only one who is reexamining the Revolution. Your urban guerrilla friend is also questioning its process. My own father, who did so much against the Batista regimen, is now being harassed by some of his customers for being too cautious about supporting the Revolution's reforms. What irony! My father, who has always opposed any dictator, feels that we now have a new master. All the signs are there."

"What about Teresita?" Pablo asked.

"Teresita feels like me," Emilio said. "The Revolución is becoming more radical and intolerant with time. Something has to be done soon or the purge will continue unabated."

Pablo agreed with Emilio that they couldn't suffer through another dictatorship.

CHAPTER XVI

The politics were once again affecting his pitching. On one sunny Sunday, he was yanked out in the third inning after allowing seven runs. As Pablo was getting ready to leave after the game, Manuel called him. "Pablo, wait. I need to talk to you."

Pablo turned around and glared at his friend.

"Are you to going to lecture me now for stinking up the place?" he said.

"Of course not. I have more important things to tell you. Let's move away from the crowd" Manuel replied in a fatherly voice.

"Pablo, you really were bad today," Manuel said, jokingly putting his arm around him. "But look at me. I have something more important to talk about. We are friends, and what I am about to tell you is confidential. Remember how happy I was celebrating the triumph of the Revolution. Well, things have changed for the worse. I have been harassed and accused of being a Yankee supporter and I don't mean supporting the Yankee team. They have even called me a *gusano*, a counterrevolutionary. They say I am collaborating with the imperialist Americans because of my connections with them after living in their country for so many years. What stupidity to make such an accusation. I am above all a Cuban who loves his country, but the Revolución is not for the people anymore, but against the people. Look at what is happening at La Cabaña fortress in Havana. Hundreds if not thousands of people are being detained and many are taken to the paredón. It could happen here too. My wife is so scared that I have contacted some relatives who live in Milwaukee. If the situation doesn't improve *pronto*, we will have to leave the country before things get out of hand. You also seem to be nervous. Your concentration and command on the mound are not good. Is something bothering you too?" Manuel asked.

"As a matter of fact, yes. I am worried about the constant surveillance and harassment. It's disgusting! What you are going through doesn't surprise me. My friend Emilio's father has been harassed too. Marcelo, of all people, has started to question the Revolution. He is considering going back to Spain before it is too late.

"But Manuel, if you leave too, what happens to my dream about playing baseball abroad?"

Manuel put his hands on Pablo's shoulders and looked him in the eye.

"Pablo, don't worry. You are my protege. You will be my number one priority as a friend and ballplayer. We will keep in touch," Manuel said.

Two months after their conversation, Manuel's body was found floating face down in the river outside Aguada with a bullet in the back of his head. It was the same river where Pablo almost drowned as a youngster when he was caught by its vortex after heavy rain and wind. Now his mentor was dead. Pablo was overcome with grief and his own bad memory of gasping for air. He finally confided in his father that he couldn't take it anymore. That he had to do something.

"Pablo, I feel your pain," his father said. "Manuel was a good friend and a great baseball mentor. He will be missed dearly, but stay calm and control your anger. Don't do anything stupid you will regret." "But Father, I don't know what to do anymore. How can I be calm! What in hell I am supposed to do? We risked our lives defending this fucking Revolución against Batista's tyranny and what we do get in return? The same crap as before. Harassment, persecution and death. The Revolution's slogan of *Patria o Muerte* is more death than anything else. Disagreeing with its ideology means prison or death, like what happened to Manuel. I don't have a future here anymore," Pablo repeated bitterly.

"Pablo, you have a future. We have the farm that your grandfather worked so hard to build. It is a very dangerous time again, but we will weather the situation. It will get better with time and you will fulfill your dream. Besides, how are you going to get out? Manuel could have helped you leave, but now he is dead," his father said.

"I don't know, I just don't know," Pablo shouted in frustration as he walked away to be alone. For the first time he did something during the weekend that he had never done before. He didn't show up on Sunday for the ball game he had been assigned to pitch. He felt like skipping school too, but his mother insisted that he go.

"Pablito mi amor you cannot miss school. The school year is almost over and soon you will be graduating. You will be the first one in the family to finish high school. There are no ands, ifs or buts about it," his mother said as she hugged him and kissed his forehead.

CHAPTER XVII

Back in school, Pablo shared his bitter feelings about Manuel's death with Emilio and Teresita. They were horrified about his assassination. Emilio spoke about his father's worry and how he was planning to get them out of Cuba.

"Father has double citizenship and has applied for a visa to Spain for the whole family. He is now waiting for it. I really don't want to go. I don't want to leave Teresita behind. I would much rather stay with her."

"Emilio, I am desperate too," Pablo said. "Maybe your father can take me."

Teresita, who was listening attentively, asked Pablo what he was thinking.

"Do you have a plan?"

"Well, I, I mean we, could leave by the sea in a *balsa* or a boat. My cousin Felipe could help us. His father was also killed by the mob and he hates this damn government. He must have some connection in Cárdenas, that seaport town near Varadero where he lives now."

"Pablo, are you serious? You must be kidding. Your plan is futile. You are really dreaming now. Cárdenas is too far away. Besides, where are we going to get the parts to make a raft or a boat? Forget about it. It is too risky."

"I agree with Teresita," Emilio said. "Taking a boat is a wild idea. Way too risky."

And then all three walked together to their hated mathematics class.

Two months later, Pablo fulfilled his promise to his mother by becoming the first one in his family to graduate from high school. However, he was surprised when he noticed that Emilio had not come to the graduation. When Pablo asked Teresita about him, she tearfully answered that he had already left with his family for Spain. She gave Pablo her address and phone number in Cienfuegos as well as Emilio's in Madrid. Then she whispered to Pablo not to forget her in his plans to leave the country.

CHAPTER XVIII

Pablo spiraled into despair, but it didn't stop there. It wasn't long after his graduation when a catastrophe struck Pablo's family. He arrived home one afternoon after baseball practice to find his cousin Lorenzo and several soldiers talking with his parents. He assumed that something must be wrong. His mother looked upset and his father's face was flushed, the large veins in his neck visibly pulsing with anger.

"Father what is going on? Why are they here?"

"My son, they have come to expropriate the farm. They want me to sign this fucking document so they can take over the farm. I will not do it," Santiago said, pointing his fingers angrily at Lorenzo and his lap dogs.

Pablo could not believe what he was hearing. He turned to his cousin and wanted an explanation.

"Lorenzo, why are you doing this? We used to be a big happy family. We grew up together, we played together. You stayed with us many times. Now you come to expropriate our family ¡*Carajo*! Don't family ties mean anything to you? Does your loyalty lie with the Revolución now? Is this what it does to people? Split families? You know that we are not rich, lazy *latifundistas*, landholders. We live off this small farm we inherited from my grandfather. Father has always helped the less fortunate whenever he could. You can verify this by asking a soldier named Ariel whose father doesn't live too far from here.

Ariel fought for the Revolución and father helped him get out of jail during the Batista regime. He also kept Ariel's family from starvation during the off season after the sugar cane harvest. Go ahead and ask him. There has to be a mistake. Talk to your superior."

But Lorenzo had it in for Pablo. He had always envied Pablo's intelligence and popularity as a baseball player. Lorenzo was a mediocre ballplayer and had a chip on his shoulder, bigger than the Brazilian Sugar Loaf Rock. He had no friends because his pettiness annoyed them.

"Pablo, here you go complaining again," Lorenzo said in a sing-song voice. "I don't give a damn how you people got the farm! We the people, the proletariats, are the Revolution. We will put an end to the abuses of the capitalist class. ¡*Coño*! There is nothing that I can do or will do. Under the National Institute of Agrarian Reform Law, it is my duty to confiscate any farm exceeding 1,000 acres so that the land is distributed among the guajiros who live and die working for rich landowners."

"Lorenzo, that's great, but I don't recall you fighting in any way against the Batista regime. Did you?"

"Of course, I did. What do you think? I didn't waste my time painting anti-government graffiti. I did more than that. If I didn't, I wouldn't be here representing the Revolución demanding you turn the farm over. And a piece of advice," Lorenzo added, his lips quivering. "Be careful what you say."

Pablo's father was indignant over the words of his hateful nephew-in-law. He couldn't contain himself anymore.

"Lorenzo, don't threaten us. What you are saying is a damn lie. And you know it. We are not a large landholder. Our farm is small. It is not bigger than three hundred acres. It is not worth a great deal. We live off what we produce, and we've exploited no one. As a matter of fact, we have always helped people in need during hard times."

"Lorenzo," his mother interjected. "I can't believe what you just said. Is this how my sister Zoila brought you up? I don't think so. She didn't teach you to be so hateful. You learned it from your shameless father. He has always envied us. Santiago has worked his tail off on this farm to feed us and even your family. After all we have done for you, you have the audacity to let the government steal the farm away from us? Lorenzo, you are nothing more than an ungrateful ingrate."

As the discussion grew hotter, the soldiers put their hands on their guns, but Lorenzo signaled them to stop. Then, he sarcastically issued an ultimatum. "*Compañero* Santiago, you either sign the document now turning the farm over to the government or we will come back later and confiscate it by any means necessary."

Santiago folded his arms and glared at Lorenzo.

"Remember, the law is the law," Lorenzo warned. "We will be back soon."

Santiago felt like running to get his shotgun, but Pablo, reading his mind, held him back. "Father, father, no, no. They will kill all of us. Let's wait and work on contingency plans."

Santiago was still fuming after Lorenzo and the soldiers left. He would have liked to join an army of peasants still fighting the government in the Escambray mountains, but he was too old and he worried about his family. His wife, knowing what was going through his mind, embraced him.

"*Mi amor*, I share your pain, but we have to be patient and have faith. There will be a way out of this horrible situation. As they say, 'When God shuts a door, He always opens a window.'"

"Victoria, what are you talking about? There's no window open for us. Don't be a fool. They will be back soon to take over the farm whether I sign this damn paper or not. Where are we going to go?" Santiago asked.

"We could move to Cárdenas where my sisters Pascuala and Josefa live. Pascuala's husband, Ignacio, has a landscape and nursery business. You are a handy man and know a lot about farming. He will hire you and the boys right away," she answered, trying to lift his spirit.

"I agree with Mother," Pablo said. "Father, I know how you feel but this sounds like a good option in case we have to leave."

Santiago snorted.

"I am telling you both that is not an option. I would rather be dead than relinquish the farm to them," he said as he stormed out of the room. Pablo's mother began to sob. Pablo hugged her, but she was inconsolable.

After Victoria gained her composure, she began to think. Maybe she could get to Lorenzo through his mother, Zoila, who still lived in Aguada. She had not talked to her sister for a while. Their families had been torn apart by the Revolution. It would be a difficult reunion but she went ahead with it anyway. She was her last hope. She arrived at Zoila's house on a sticky, hot summer day. She knocked at the door several times, but nobody answered. Then she walked to the back of the house where she found Zoila in the garden watering the flowers. As soon as she saw her younger sister, she ran toward her and they embraced effusively. Victoria could hardly contain her emotion as she broke into tears.

"Victoria, what is wrong? How can I help you? Victoria told her sister about the confrontation they had at the farm with the government. "Zoila, our families might disagree about the Revolution, but you are my sister. I hope you can help us. Lorencito came to talk to us yesterday with several soldiers to confiscate our farm. He asked Santiago to sign a document to make the takeover official. He refused to do it. Then Lorencito threatened us. He told us he was coming back in a few days to take it over no matter what. Zoila, I am terrified about what might happen. I don't know what to do. I am sorry to burden you with our problems, but you are our last hope. Please talk to Lorencito. Maybe he would talk to his superiors."

"Victoria, stop crying. Control yourself. I thought something was wrong when Lorencito stopped by last night. I heard him talking with his father about your farm. He was pissed off. He kept swearing and screaming about how stupid Santiago was. Lorencito has always been a difficult child. He is like his father. A manipulator. Power has gone to his head, especially now in the aftermath of the Revolution. It is his way or the highway. But don't worry. He will hear from me when he returns tomorrow. I will do everything to help you. I love you no matter what. Stop worrying. Everything will be okay." Both sisters embraced again, and Victoria thanked her sister profusely.

CHAPTER XIX

Several weeks passed and nothing happened. Then late one afternoon Lorenzo showed up. He came back to the farm with several soldiers, and his friend Ariel was one of them. Lorenzo called out for Santiago several times. The whole family came out of the house to meet him, except for Pablo, who decided to stay in the kitchen, out of sight from his temperamental cousin.

"Santiago, I have a new document for you to sign," Lorenzo said. "It is different than the other one I left before. The government will still own the farm but you can stay as a supervisor. You are lucky that our compañero Ariel and others have vouched for you. He confirmed that you got him out of jail during the repressive Batista regimen and helped his family many times."

"What does it mean to be a supervisor?" Santiago asked.

"Read the document. The farm will be run as a cooperative. Profits will be supervised and crops will be planted for the benefit of the people. I will return in a few days," Lorenzo said as he got in the government jeep and drove away.

Pablo's father was still mad as a hornet after they left. He was adamant about not signing any paper. Why should he be a supervisor? The farm was a legacy of his father and belonged to his family, not to the fucking government. Pablo's mother was more conciliatory.

"Santiago, mi amor, this is not the best solution, but at least we could stay on the farm. Otherwise, we will have to move. Think about it."

"Victoria, for Christ's sake! Listen to what I have to say. I will not turn the farm over to the government and become its supervisor. This is a ruse. A damn lie. Today I am the supervisor, and tomorrow I will be fired," he said as he stomped out of the house and headed toward the barn.

Pablo had heard every word of his cousin's second threat and felt angrier than he thought possible. Losing the farm to a power-grabbing government was wrong and the ultimate insult to his family. He had finally had it! There was no future for him in this godforsaken place.

Pablo began to plan to leave the country as many others had done already. He thought about Marcelo and his family in Madrid. Maybe there was a way Marcelo could help get them get to the U.S. by going through Spain? After all, his paternal grandfather had migrated from Galicia. With this in mind, Pablo went to Aguada one morning to call Marcelo from the *Centralita Teléfonica*, the town's telephone station. At a signal from the switchboard operator, Pablo was connected. He was careful about what he said on the phone, aware that the government routinely monitored personal calls to other countries. Nevertheless, he did ask Marcelo to look into the possibility of getting an entry visa to Spain for them as he did for his family. Marcelo promised him that he would try. He said he would call back at the same time in two weeks with an answer. Pablo paid for the call and then went to practice with his baseball team.

He saw Ariel at the sidelines, watching him pitch. Pablo was surprised to see him. After the practice, Ariel walked toward him, but Pablo wasn't sure if he wanted to talk to him after what happened at the farm.

"Pablo, I was watching you. You are good, brother. You are better than ever. Baseball is your future. Anyhow, I came to talk to you because you are my friend. I owe you an apology for what happened the other day at your place. I went to the farm because I couldn't disobey the wicked Lorenzo's order. Man, he is drunk with power. The way he talked to your father was disrespectful.

Lorenzo has a vendetta against your family. He knows that your father is not a big landowner, but he doesn't give a damn. He is too hateful. He harassed your family out of spite and to show his power. I want you to know that he asked my father to supervise the farm, but he refused to do it. His answer was that he was not competent and would destroy the farmland. Pablo, I am no longer your baseball buddy, but I will always be your friend no matter what happens."

"Ariel, I really appreciate your apology. It means a lot to me. I trust you. I always counted on you as my dear friend," Pablo said as they shook hands.

Back at the farm, Pablo found out from his mother that his father had finally signed the document.

"Pablito, it took a lot, but I was able to convince your father, for the good of the family, to give up the farm. He is a very unhappy man now. I worry about him."

Pablo and his mother knew that their simple and peaceful life on the farm would change for the worse, but it was the best decision for now.

When Pablo spoke with Marcelo again, there was more bad news. He told Pablo that the official at the

Cuban Embassy in Madrid had treated him very badly when he asked about the possibility of getting a visa for a family who had Spanish relatives. The functionary replied in a nasty tone of voice that only Cuba could decide who may leave the island. Then he added that anyone given permission to leave Cuba would have to wait at least three years, not be allowed to work while waiting and the Cuban government would confiscate everything he owned after he left.

The Spanish government's reply to his inquiry wasn't very encouraging either. According to them, one could only apply if he had dual citizenship as Marcelo did. Pablo thanked Marcelo for all he had done. He sent his good wishes to the family. He finally told Marcelo to tell Emilio that Teresita missed him, but that she was hoping to join him soon.

Despite the bad news, Pablo refused to be discouraged. He had to persevere and rise above this situation. There had to be another alternative, another way to escape to freedom, maybe by sea. The Revolución was a fraud. People were trying to escape by boats, balsas, or any other means. He damn well could too.

After Lorenzo returned to the farm to pick up the signed document of expropriation, Pablo talked to his parents about visiting his aunt Pascuala in Cárdenas and see how her husband Ignacio's landscape and nursery business was doing. He didn't tell them he was going to ask him for a job and talk to Josefa's son, Felipe, to help him to leave the country on a raft or by boat.

CHAPTER XX

When Pablo arrived in Cárdenas, he loved it. Despite its size, he was impressed with its cultural offerings and its 19th century buildings splashed across the city. He was looking forward to visiting the house of José Antonio Echevarría, who was murdered at the University of Havana in1957 by Batista's goons while defending democracy. He also wanted to visit the Arechabala Rum Refinery known for its Havana Club rum. it wasn't long before he started working part-time at Ignacio's business and found out what his cousin Felipe thought about the Revolution.

They were having a beer at the *Taberna Corona* and Pablo worked up the courage to bring up his father's murder.

"I feel for you, man. it must have been tough to move after they killed your father. Have you made some friends here?" Pablo asked.

"Oh yeah, it was hard. I hated my mother for leaving Aguada, but to tell you the truth we couldn't stay there after my father's murder. We feared for our lives and had to move away. My father was a good man. He never harassed or killed anybody. In fact, he had quietly helped many people. You don't know how much I despise this shitty Revolution. Pascuala and Ignacio have been a great help. They helped us at a very difficult time in our lives. Ignacio hired me part-time to work at his store just like he did you. I also do some work with a fishing crew. I like to fish and it's a nice way to relax. But I don't have many friends. I feel isolated here, like a pariah. But Pablo, what about you? Why did you leave? Why aren't you playing baseball anymore?" Felipe asked.

"Well, you don't know how many bad things have happened since you left. The government confiscated our farm as it has done with so many other properties. I don't know if you have heard, but even baseball icons like Orestes Miñoso and Sandy Amorós, who are from here, didn't escape the wrath of Fidel Castro. Amorós, for example, fell into disgrace when he returned to Cuba after the triumph of the Revolución to get his family out. His refusal to manage a Cuban national team cost him dearly. He lost everything here, all his properties. Well, we lost our farm too. The expropriation was ugly. Our cousin Lorenzo was the ringleader. He is a prime example of what the Revolución can do. It has even divided our family. After father refused to hand over the farm, Lorenzo came back a second time. He had the nerve to ask father to manage the farm the government was stealing from him. How humiliating! Father would have killed all of them, if he could have. Mother finally convinced him to accept the supervisor job for the good of the family.

"So, I need to tell you the truth. I came here looking for freedom. I thought you might help me to escape."

"But Pablo, what about your baseball dream? Felipe asked again.

"My dream is on hold for now, but I know it could never happen here. Who knows if it will ever happen? Only time will tell. My mentor Manuel was murdered, just like your father. His body was dumped in the river in Aguada where we used to go swimming. Felipe, I don't have a future here anymore. I have to escape this rat hole. Some of my friends have already left by whatever means they were able to find. Could you help me make a *balsa* or build a boat to escape this nightmare with my friend Teresita?" Pablo pleaded.

"I'd like to, but I'm not sure I can," Felipe said. "Look Pablo, if I agree to help, how and where are we going to find the materials? Even if we find them, we don't have the skills to make a balsa or build a boat.

Besides, we have to be extremely careful. There are too many *chivatos* around here. Cárdenas is a small city and everyone knows everybody. If people get wind of what we're planning, we will be killed or put in jail for a long time. By the way, who is Teresita? A girlfriend?" Felipe asked with a mischievous look in his eyes.

"Teresita is Emilio's girlfriend. He is a friend who left Cuba. He lives in Madrid now with his family. We all went to high school in Cienfuegos. Teresita wants to escape with us. Then Emilio could come to the United States or she could try to join him in Madrid."

After another beer, Felipe smiled and agreed to help.

"But look, Pablo, there is no guarantee."

CHAPTER XXI

Indeed, Pablo and Felipe became frustrated with the passing of time and lack of results. They couldn't find the rafting materials they needed, and Felipe was ready to quit.

"Look Pablo, this is not going well at all. Ignacio already suspects something. He questioned me the other day why I was scavenging around the store. He wondered why I needed some plastic and an inner tube he had thrown away. I told him that I wanted to take them when I go fishing with my buddies. Ignacio wouldn't turn us in, but he would stop our plan immediately. He will think we are crazy trying to escape in a flimsy raft or an unsafe boat. Besides, forget about finding a carpenter we can trust. We would be dead meat."

Pablo understood his cousin's fears, but he refused to give up. He suggested Felipe check with his fishing crew. They might know someone willing to sell an old boat. Bingo! Two weeks later Felipe had good news. One of the men told him he saw a sign for sale for a rickety boat in the fishing town of Boca de Camarioca. Pablo and Felipe went to see it. They met the owner, a likeable and energetic older fisherman, named Eufemio and his granddaughter Marisol. She was a cheerful young lady with long black hair and hazel eyes, which were glancing quite a bit toward Pablo. He guessed she was eighteen, his age. He liked that she was pretty and a little shorter than him.

He turned his attention back to the boat. He cited all of its deficiencies as they decided on its worth and they finally agreed on a price. However, they could only give a down payment. They assured the fisherman they would be back with the rest of the money in the coming weeks. The fisherman took the down payment and agreed to repair the boat for an extra amount of money. He told them he would have the boat fixed and ready to take to sea in a few weeks.

Pablo and Felipe thought that the purchasing price and cost of repair were fair but wondered where they were going to get the rest of the money. Pablo also kept thinking about the fisherman's granddaughter. He understood now what his grandfather Quintín meant when he told him about "love at first sight" upon meeting his grandmother in a verbena. They returned the following week with the money from their savings and with an advance payment from Ignacio, who could also use the boat when he went fishing. However, Pablo kept coming back with the pretext of seeing the progress Eufemio was making with the repairs. What he really wanted was to talk to Marisol. Pablo always felt comfortable being around her and couldn't keep her out of his mind. On one of his visits, she told him about herself and her family.

CHAPTER XXII

"Pablo, my parents are dead. Eufemio is my grandfather. He and sweet Nana Rosa raised me. Sadly, *abuelita* also died several years ago of a massive stroke. Pablo, you know what else? Like you, I finished high school and would like to continue studying at the university level. However, I am facing many obstacles because I am a Catholic. My belief in Jesus Christ, our Lord, is very important to me. My goal is to become a pediatrician, but I will never compromise my faith for this atheistic government."

"Marisol, I am so sorry to hear about the deaths of your parents and grandma. But I am elated to hear how you feel about our government. I am also troubled by its dictatorial ways. I have lost my faith in the Revolution. It is one lie after another. I believe in freedom, and we don't have it anymore. I won't be able to fulfill my dream of playing professional baseball by staying here."

Pablo reached out and took Marisol's hands into his own.

"Marisol, I really liked you from the first moment I saw you. We have so much in common. Maybe we could achieve our goals together," Pablo said, anxiously watching for her reaction.

"Pablo, I really like you too, but what do you mean by achieving our goals together?" she asked with a smile.

"I mean we could escape together" Pablo answered, squeezing her hands.

"That is crazy, just crazy," she said. Then suddenly she kissed him softly on the lips and moved away when her grandfather called her.

"Grandfather, I am coming," she answered and ran to meet him.

Marisol's grandfather was stern as he warned her to be careful.

"*Mi niña*, my sweet Marisol, I saw you kissing Pablo. What are you doing? You don't know him. He is not from here. I am telling you to be careful."

"Grandpa, Pablo is a nice guy. I like him. We have a lot in common. He loves freedom like me. He dreams of becoming a big-time baseball player like I dream about becoming a doctor. Don't worry, Grandpa. I will be careful," she said as she tenderly kissed him on the cheek

Felipe was furious when he heard what Pablo had told Marisol.

"Pablo, you moron. Are you stupid, man? Think about what you have done. Don't be a fool. As far as we know, she could have already told her grandfather about our plans to escape. Then he could have told someone else. We are in trouble man," he shouted.

"Felipe, don't be so angry. I understand you're scared, but I trust her. I know deep in my heart that she loves me and would be willing to escape with us to fulfill her dream too. Even if she were to talk to her grandfather, it would be to ask him for his help. Don't you agree that his experience would be valuable?" Pablo asked, hoping that Felipe would be more understanding.

But Felipe kept ranting.

"Pablo, wake up! You are dreaming. You just met her. You are letting your emotions control your reasoning. I am so worried about escaping. I haven't thought about telling anybody, not even my mother. Are you going to tell your parents?" Felipe asked.

His question made Pablo uneasy. He had intended to tell his parents about his decision to escape but just kept forgetting—sort of.

"I do plan to tell my parents, but you are too nervous, Felipe. Lighten up a bit! Everything will be okay. Soon we will be out of this rat hole. We will be free like birds to do what we want and to express how we feel," Pablo assured his cousin.

CHAPTER XXIII

A few days later, Pablo spoke with Ignacio about visiting his parents. It was a difficult visit in many ways. When he arrived home, it bothered him to see that his proud father had become a shadow of himself. He was depressed and seemed to go through the motions of caring for the farm. They had stolen not only his farm but his dignity as well. Most of the supervision and work on the farm was now done by his two older brothers. Pablo's mother was more upbeat despite the pain of watching her husband slowly sink into his depression.

Pablo returned to tell his parents about his decision to escape, but was concerned about how they might react. In the meantime, he decided to go to the telephone station in Aguada to call Teresita. He asked the operator to connect him. After several rings, Teresita came on the line. "Hello, hello, who is calling please?"

"Teresita, this is Pablo. I am calling from Aguada."

Speaking in code, Pablo asked her to come to Cárdenas for their final fishing outing in Playa Larga.

What he really meant was for her to get ready to leave the country.

"Teresita, we are all looking forward to this final fishing trip. I know you're a keen fan of fishing and would love it. You don't want to miss it. Will you be able to come?"

There was a long pause. Finally, Teresita began talking, her voice choking up.

"Pablo, I am sorry. I would love to come, but I can't. Emilio died unexpectedly several weeks ago in a traffic accident. He was returning to Madrid from a trip to the town of El Escorial when someone coming in the opposite direction crossed the lane and crashed head on against them." Teresita was sobbing now. "No one survived. I am devastated. I don't know what to do anymore. Please pray for me."

Pablo was nearly speechless in shock. He tried to think of something to say that would be remotely comforting to his friend.

"Teresita, I am so sorry to hear about Emilio's death. You both were so close. Emilio was a great friend. At least we will always have great memories of him. Nobody can take that away from us. I wish

I could be there with you, but I have to return to Cárdenas in a few days. I am working now at my uncle Ignacio's landscape store, but I'm always home at night. Please call me. Anytime. My thoughts and prayers are with you."

CHAPTER XXIV

On the last day with his family, Pablo finally decided it was time to level with his parents.

"Dad and Mom, what I am about to tell you is difficult, but I have to be truthful with you. Please understand. I love both of you dearly, but I have decided to leave the country. As father liked to tell me, politics is like a yoyo; things will get better with time. Well, they haven't. We are the in the same situation or worse than we were with the murderous Batista regimen. We are miserable. I have lost my faith in the Revolution. We are systematically being destroyed little by little every day. Look what happened to Aunt Josefa's husband, to my mentor Manuel, and, for that matter, how they stole our farm. It is happening all over the country. Who or what is next? I don't know. But I do know that I can't hold much hope. I know I don't have a future here anymore as a baseball player unless I support their tyranny. I love freedom and I won't do that," Pablo said.

He waited anxiously to hear what they had to say. His mother's reaction was as expected. She was very upset and couldn't believe what she heard. She wanted to know more about this dangerous escape and who was leaving with him.

"Pablito, my boy, what are you thinking? What you are planning to do is crazy. Please, for the love of God, reconsider your decision. I can't believe you are going to leave us. Who is helping you?" she asked tearfully.

"Mother, Felipe is coming as well as Marisol. She is a girl I met in Cárdenas. I have fallen in love with her. Like me she wants to escape. Her dream is to become a doctor in a free country. Her grandfather is a fisherman. He is fixing a boat we bought from him. He might help us to escape too. I am sorry mother, but I cannot stay in this country under our land-stealing, murderous government any longer. Once I get back to Cárdenas, we will leave any day. Please, don't tell anyone else, even Israel or Alberto or the girls. They could innocently tell someone and we would be in a lot of trouble" Pablo pleaded.

His mother asked if Felipe's mother knew his plan to
leave too.

"I don't know. He feels like me, but it is up to him to decide what to do."

Then his father, who had been quietly listening, spoke.

"Pablo, my son, I understand your decision. You have always expressed yourself clearly about freedom and human rights. You are a grown man who definitely knows what he wants. You remind me of your grandfather, who left his own country at a young age to escape famine and turmoil for a better life. Pablo, there is not much to do on our stolen farm. You have a future ahead of you. It is up to you, my son. Go ahead and God protect you and the young lady you love."

Even though Pablo's mother feared she would never see her son again—what she considered the ultimate sacrifice. Yet she decided to bless him and send him on his way. After all, she wanted the best for him.

"Pablito, here is a medallion of Cachita. May she protect you in your courageous journey." As her eyes filled with tears, she tenderly hugged him.

The morning he was to take the train back to Cárdenas, his old friend Ariel was also at the station. It was early, and the sun was red and low on the horizon.

"Hey buddy!" Ariel said. "I heard that you moved to Cárdenas to work at your uncle's business. I miss seeing you around and wanted to talk to you before you went back. As you saw, your father is not doing very well. He is not himself. He is still being hounded by the idiot Lorenzo. I wanted to let you know that I am doing all I can to help him. Also, I wanted to tell you that your recent call to a girl named Teresita in Cienfuegos was monitored. You invited her to join you on a fishing trip to Playa Larga. Is she coming?" Ariel asked casually.

Pablo's response was carefully worded to dispel any suspicion in his friend's mind, but alarms were ringing in his head. How could Ariel know about the phone call unless someone on the inside the government tipped him off?

"Teresita is a friend I went to high school with in Cienfuegos. She loves fishing and I thought she might like to join us. Cárdenas is known for good fishing year around, but, I don't think she will be able to come. By the way, I already met a beautiful girl in Cárdenas who I like a lot," Pablo said with a smile.

"I know. The Revolución has many eyes and ears. You are my best friend and I want you to be careful," Ariel warned him.

"Ariel, you heard right. I returned to tell my parents about moving to Cárdenas and to pick up a few things I left behind like my old pitching glove.

I am not coming back for a while. Cárdenas is a beautiful city. Come and visit me. You are most welcome," Pablo said.

They hugged and Pablo said one last good-bye to his closest friend—a friend he now couldn't fully trust.

CHAPTER XXV

After his return to Cárdenas, in addition to his job, there were many other things to do. He wanted to talk to Marisol's grandfather and see how the boat repair was coming along and to help Felipe to get the materials they would need for their escape. But more than anything else, he was dying to see Marisol. Marisol also missed Pablo badly. Felipe said that every time he visited the boatyard, she'd ask him when Pablo would be back.

As soon as he returned, Pablo went to see her. They met and kissed passionately. Marisol told him she had made up her mind.

"Pablo, I missed you a lot. I cannot live without you. I have decided to escape with you and Felipe. I feel like the biblical Ruth. Where you go Pablo, I will go. Your people are my people. I haven't told grandfather yet about leaving, but he suspects that something is going on. I asked when the boat would be ready to take to sea and he wondered why I needed to know. I hinted about leaving by telling him that we were planning a special fishing trip and he could join us. He said he would love to go along. I feel in my heart that grandfather knows and will help us to escape. He likes you and wants the best for us."

Pablo was spellbound listening to Marisol talk. He kissed her again and told her how happy she made him.

"Marisol, I am so fortunate that I met you. I feel so at ease with you. We were born for each other. We are soul mates." Then they went looking for her grandfather.

"Grandfather, grandfather, Pablo is back. He wants to talk to you," Marisol shouted as she and Pablo went searching for him.

"What is all this racket about," Eufemio asked as he came out from his workshop.

"Mr. Villareal, I came to find out when the boat will be ready to take to sea, but more importantly I came to ask for the hand of your granddaughter. Marisol and I love each other deeply and want to be together forever," Pablo spoke with assurance and sincerity.

"Yes, yes. Marisol has told to me how much you love each other. That is good. Love, faith, and trust are the most important things in a lasting relationship. Pablo, you are a fine young man. I appreciate you asking me to approve of your relationship with my sweet granddaughter. I do, but first of all, I need to know your immediate plans. How are you going to support her if you get married? I don't see you as a fisherman, and you only have a part-time job now. You cannot live only on love especially when the children come," Eufemio said, looking intensely at both of them.

"Well, I could get a job farming. I grew up on a farm. I know a lot about farming. But we have bigger dreams. As you know, she wants to be a doctor, but she is having trouble being accepted at the university because of her religious beliefs. I plan to be a major league baseball player when we get up north, to the United States" Pablo said knowing that perhaps he had revealed too much of their plan in his reply.

"Pablo, thank you for your honesty. That is what I suspected when Marisol hinted about your plan. Okay. Are you going to use the boat I am repairing for you?"

At this moment, Marisol winked at Pablo and jumped into the conversation to support him. "Grandpa, you know his answer."

"Of course, I do. I just wanted to hear it from him. Marisol, you are my treasure. You are the only thing I have left in this life. I will do anything to help both of you to reach your goals. By the way Pablo, call me

Eufemio from now on. Welcome to our little family!” he said and got up to hug him.

CHAPTER XXVI

Eufemio told them it would take longer to fix the boat now. He had to find a good motor somewhere for navigating the treacherous Caribbean currents. He also needed a compass, floating devices, and plenty of gasoline. He knew they would be risky to get and conceal these items from the government, but he would get them.

Everyone was anxious as they waited for the day to escape. In the meantime, Eufemio kept working on the boat. He finally bought the motor and the compass he was looking for on the black market. He now had to discuss the logistics of the escape plan and pick the day and time when they could leave. Three days before leaving, Teresita showed up at Pablo's work with a little suitcase. He was surprised to see her again and took her to the shade of a tree to talk.

"Did you change your mind?" he asked, worriedly.

"I did! Emilio believed in freedom as much as I do. He would want me to escape with you."

Pablo was elated and hugged her tightly.

"This is wonderful, Teresita! You'll have to hide until we leave. I think the government is keeping an eye on us—and you."

He took Teresita to Hostal Rodrigo, not too far from his uncle's store. It was a modest building—not too expensive with few customers. Nevertheless, Pablo told her to keep a low profile. He would come back in the evening with his cousin Felipe to pick her up to go to a meeting at Eufemio's house to discuss the escape plan.

At the meeting, Eufemio explained what to do and when they would be able to leave. "I know you are all apprehensive about this dangerous trip, but relax. I have been around the sea all my life. I respect the sea, but I know it like the back of my hand. Fear not. Everything will be okay. Now listen carefully to my instructions. Today is Friday. We are going to leave next Monday early in the morning from Playa Larga near the docks. It is not very far from here. Be there early. I mean no later than 5:00 a.m. Marisol and I will be nearby, pretending to be fishing. If we are questioned by the Border Patrol agents, we have a fishing permit. Pablo, Felipe and Teresita, you'll stay by the rocks and pretend to be fishing near Vista Alegre beach, which is also close to the docks. There might be a few swimmers and some fishermen around, even that early, but don't worry. Everything will be okay. You'll find the fishing poles, bait and sombreros hidden by the big rock. You cannot miss it. Be discreet. Marisol and I will pick you up. We will have everything else we need in the boat. We have plenty of water, but it wouldn't hurt if you bring your own bottle. Believe me. It will get hot and you will be thirsty. Any questions?"

Felipe wanted to know why he had picked Monday and not Saturday or Sunday.

"Son, I picked Monday because the forecast is for mostly clear weather for the day with a few showers. The weather here is unpredictable, but that is the forecast. Also, on Monday, many locals won't be around after being forced to attend the 26 of July celebration," he said sarcastically.

Eufemio finished by telling them to follow the instructions carefully, have faith, and to ask God for his protection.

CHAPTER XXVII

Pablo, Felipe and Teresita came early to the beach to get the fishing gear that Eufemio had hidden by the big rock. As Eufemio predicted, there was hardly anybody around except for a few locals frolicking on the beach and some fishermen. Two hours ticked by and there was no sight of Marisol and her grandfather. Everyone was on edge. They were worried, fearful that something might have happened. Then, out of the blue, a tall young soldier with a slight limp appeared walking toward them. Everyone froze, except Pablo. He could not believe who he was seeing. It was Ariel. He greeted everybody and asked to talk to Pablo.

"My dear friend Pablo, have you finally become a fisherman? As I told you, the Revolución has many eyes and ears. You cannot get away from me, man. I thought something was fishy when we saw each other at the train station in Aguada. Also, your call to your friend Teresita inviting her to join you on a unique fishing trip was weird when you have never been a fisherman. Anyhow, they have been tracking you for a while. I volunteered to help. I arrived yesterday and was told to keep an eye on you. Your girlfriend

Marisol and her grandfather are not here because they were detained by the Border Patrol officers."

Pablo gasped. How could his best friend betray him!

"Don't worry," Ariel said, seeing the look on his friend's face. "After being questioned, they were allowed to continue fishing. They should be here at any time to pick us up. I said us, because I am escaping too if you take me. I have seen the monster, the Revolution, inside out and I hate it. When we reach the other shore, I could also have freedom and maybe be your baseball buddy again. Is that okay Pablo?" he asked with a grin.

"Ariel, I am astonished. You are a true friend. You could have crushed our dream, but you chose to help us. We are so grateful to you. Of course, you can come with us and fulfill your dream too," Pablo said. "Welcome to our great escape!"

It wasn't long before Eufemio and Marisol arrived to pick them up. "I am sorry we are a little bit late, but we were stopped and interrogated by the Border Patrol goons. They finally let us go because this young man helped us," Eufemio said, pointing at Ariel.

"We are old friends," Pablo said. "He has been my baseball buddy since we started playing in pickup games in elementary school. He is coming with us too. Eufemio, do we have room for him?" Pablo asked.

"Of course, we do. He is more than welcome. Are we ready to leave on our fishing trip now?" he asked with a big smile. They ran with some trepidation towards the boat that would take them across the unpredictable and dangerous Straits of Florida. Eufemio had done a magnificent job on the old boat. He replaced the worn out planks, fixed some damage in the bow and stern and sealed and coated every piece of the boat. He finally installed a reconstructed motor and a propeller and made sure they worked. The old boat was now ready to sail.

CHAPTER XXVIII

It was a sunny day as forecast when they started their journey. A slight breeze cooled the rising temperature. They were accompanied at the beginning by a school of fish of beautiful colors, shapes and sizes. The next few hours were nerve racking as they tried to avoid the Cuban Border Patrol agents. Eufemio told everybody to lay flat in the boat, except for him and Marisol to give the appearance that they were fishing as the boat slowly moved away from Cuban shore. They cheered and hollered the moment they were in international waters, out of the grasp of the Border Patrol agents. At sunset, the weather suddenly changed for the worse. It rained heavily and the wind roared like a lion. They were terrified. The storm was so strong that the boat was like a bouncing ball as big waves crashed against it. They had to bail out water with a bucket. After several hours, the fury of the sea abated. It became pitch black and The temperature dropped to twenty degrees. They were drenched and exhausted. Some of them slept curled up in the bottom of the boat, huddling together for warmth, as it moved with the current.

The next day, the sunrise was stunning. The temperature began to rise and it became hot very quickly. They ate some of the food, mostly crackers and peanuts. Teresita pointed to several sharks swimming alongside the boat.

"Hit the sharks on the head with the paddles if they get too close and bump the boat," Eufemio said.

The sharks appeared and disappeared for a while, like they were eyeing them for lunch. In late afternoon, the weather changed quickly. It became overcast. Strong winds pushed the boat around until evening and a heavy rain came and went. They spent another cold night under a moonless, starless sky. They felt unmoored in the sea of black. They took turns laying on the floor of the boat, covering themselves with plastic sheets, and slept fitfully.

The following day the sea was mostly calm until noon when all hell broke loose. An explosion jolted them. The motor blew up damaging part of the bow. The boat began to take on water rapidly. They worked feverishly to stem the flow. They lost everything. Eufemio cursed at losing the compass and the bad motor.

"Damnit! I should not have trusted that son-of-a-bitch Bartolo. He sold me this worthless motor. It is a piece of shit."

Panic set in as the boat drifted aimlessly for hours as Eufemio tried to fix it. Fortunately, the weather stayed calm for several hours. But at sunset it changed again. The wind began to whip up furiously. It became cloudy and there was a heavy downpour. Huge waves spun the boat around. They had to hang onto a rope and to each other to avoid falling into the sea. Marisol lost hold of the rope and was thrown overboard. Pablo jumped over to save her.

Eufemio began to scream when he saw them struggling against enormous waves. Pablo thought of just how cold the water was, his desperation to find Marisol, just before he lost consciousness.

Eufemio jumped out to help, but he too was swallowed by the angry sea. Water kept gushing in through the damaged bow. Teresita kept holding on to the rope while Ariel and Felipe tried to control the boat. They were terrified and feared for their lives in the dark of the night. The wind kept howling and enormous waves continued crashing against the boat. The two men were finally swept away by one of the gigantic waves, while Teresita clung to the rope.

Days later, the Coast Guard reported that a female Cuban immigrant was rescued from an unsafe boat that capsized near Islamorada. She was found semiconscious, dehydrated, and her skin was sunburned and covered with blisters. She was taken to a local hospital where she is recovering. She reported that she was with five others, "good friends" who perished in the sea.

EPILOGUE

Teresita was lucky to survive the attempt to cross the Straits of Florida seeking freedom. It was a miracle that she didn´t drown or get eaten by sharks as many others were in this repeated tragedy. She misses Emilio terribly and often thinks about her friends.

For the first time, she is sitting in the hospital courtyard on a beautiful summer day recovering from her ordeal. A plethora of fragrant flowers, colorful butterflies and chirping birds reminds her of Cuba, and her eyes fill with tears. She feels alone in many ways, but looks forward to a future of hope and blessings in a free country. Her goal is to become a journalist. As the only survivor of this tragic escape, she wants people to remember not only her brave friends, but the many others fleeing oppression and tyranny. Even though many of them perished, she'll be sure their ideas and deeds are not forgotten.

GLOSSARY

Abuelita: Affectionate form used for grandmother.
Alacranes: Scorpions
Balsa: Raft
Barbudos: Bearded men, rebel forces
Bodega: Grocery store
Cachita: Affectionate name given to Our Lady of Charity
Cabrones: Bastards
Canallas: Scoundrels
¡Carajo! Damn, fuck
Central Perseverancia: Sugar mill Perseverancia
Chivatos: Informers, snitches
Compañeros: Comrades
¡Coño! Damnit!
Día de los Reyes Magos: Three Kings´Day
Dígame: One way of answering the phone in Cuba
Entra. Come in
Esbirros: Henchmen, goons
Galleguito: Diminutive of Gallego, a person from Galicia, Spain. Generic term for a Spaniard in Cuba.
Guajiros: Countrymen, peasants

Gusano: Worm, deserter counterrevolutionary

Instituto de Segunda Enseñanza: High school

La Cueva: The cave

Latifundistas: Landholders

La Virgen de la Caridad del Cobre: Our Lady of Charity. Cuba´s patron Saint.

Libertad: Freedom

Marabú: Sicklebush

Mi amor: Sweetheart, honey

Mima: Another way of calling mom in Cuba

Mi niña: My little girl

Oshún: The goddess of love, beauty and wealth in the Yoruba religion. The Lucumí Venus is one of the most popular and loved divinity in the Afro-Cuban Santería religion. Her followers identify her with the Lady of Charity, patron saint of Cuba, and call her affectionally Cachita.

Pablito: The diminutive in Spanish also conveys a sense of intimacy or endearment.

Pachanga: Party, a festive time

Paredón: To the wall to be shot

Patria o Muerte: Fatherland or Death

Querido: My dear
Revolución: Revolution
Soplón: Informer
Taberna: Tavern
Tiempo muerto: Dead season for sugar cane
¡Vamos! Let's go
Verbena: Town's festival
Zafra: Sugar-cane harvest and milling